An
UNEXPECTED

Christmas

GIFT

AN **AMISH CHRISTMAS MIRACLES** STORY

JENNIFER SPREDEMANN

© 2020, 2021 by Jennifer Spredemann, J.E.B. Spredemann

Copyright. All rights reserved. No part of this work/book may be copied, transmitted, or stored in any form or by any means, except for brief quotations in printed reviews, without prior written consent from the authors/publisher.

All incidents and characters in this book are completely fictional and derived by the author's imagination. Any resemblance to actual incidents and persons living or dead are purely coincidental.

Published in Indiana by *Blessed Publishing*.

www.jenniferspredemann.com

All Scripture quotations are taken from the *King James Version*

of the *Holy Bible.*

Cover design by *iCreate Designs* ©

ISBN: 978-1-940492-71-1

10 9 8 7 6 5 4 3 2 1

Get a FREE short story as my thank you gift when you sign up for my newsletter here: www.jenniferspredemann.com

BOOKS by JENNIFER SPREDEMANN

AMISH BY ACCIDENT TRILOGY

Amish by Accident

*Englisch on Purpose (*Prequel to *Amish by Accident)*

*Christmas in Paradise (*Sequel to *Amish by Accident*) (co-authored with Brandi Gabriel)

AMISH SECRETS SERIES

An Unforgivable Secret - Amish Secrets 1

A Secret Encounter - Amish Secrets 2

A Secret of the Heart - Amish Secrets 3

An Undeniable Secret - Amish Secrets 4

A Secret Sacrifice - Amish Secrets 5 (co-authored with Brandi Gabriel)

A Secret of the Soul - Amish Secrets 6

A Secret Christmas – Amish Secrets 2.5 (co-authored with Brandi Gabriel)

AMISH BIBLE ROMANCES

An Amish Reward (Isaac)

An Amish Deception (Jacob)

An Amish Honor (Joseph)

An Amish Blessing (Ruth)

An Amish Betrayal (David)

AMISH COUNTRY BRIDES

The Trespasser (Amish Country Brides)

The Heartbreaker (Amish Country Brides)

The Charmer (Amish Country Brides)

The Drifter (Amish Country Brides)

The Giver (Amish Country Brides Christmas)

The Teacher (Amish Country Brides)

The Widower (Amish Country Brides)

The Keeper (Amish Country Brides)

FAIRY TALES

The Princess and the Prayer Kapp (Cindy's Story & Rosabelle's Story)

OTHER

Learning to Love – Saul's Story (Sequel to Chloe's Revelation)

Love Impossible

Unlikely Santa

Unlikely Sweethearts

An Unexpected Christmas Gift (Amish Christmas Miracles Collection)

COMING 2021 (Lord Willing)

The Pretender (Amish Country Brides)

Unlikely Singing (More Amish Christmas Miracles)

COMING 2022 (Lord Willing)

Title TBD (Amish Spring Romance collection)

BOOKS by J.E.B. SPREDEMANN

AMISH GIRLS SERIES

Joanna's Struggle

Danika's Journey

Chloe's Revelation

Susanna's Surprise

Annie's Decision

Abigail's Triumph

Brooke's Quest

Leah's Legacy

A Christmas of Mercy – Amish Girls Holiday

Unofficial Glossary of Pennsylvania Dutch Words

Ach – Oh

Aenti – Aunt

Boppli/Bopplin – Baby/Babies

Bruder/Brieder – Brother/Brothers

Chust – Just

Daed/Dat – Dad

Dawdi – Grandfather

Dawdi haus – A small dwelling typically used for grandparents

Denki – Thanks

Der Herr – The Lord

Dochder(n) – Daughter(s)

Dummkopp – Dummy

Englischer – A non-Amish person

Ferhoodled – Crazy, scatterbrained, mind is elsewhere

Fraa – Wife/Missus

G'may – Members of an Amish fellowship

Gott – God

Gross sohn – Grandson

Gut – Good

Guten tag – Good day, good morning

Herr – Mister/Lord

Jah – Yes

Kapp – Amish head covering

Kinner – Children

Kumm – Come

Maed/Maedel – Girls/Girl

Mamm – Mom

Rumspringa – Running around period for Amish youth

Schatzi – Sweetheart

Schweschder(n) – Sister(s)

Sohn – Son

Wunderbaar – Wonderful

Author's Note

The Amish/Mennonite people and their communities differ one from another. There are, in fact, no two Amish communities exactly alike. It is this premise on which this book is written. I have taken cautious steps to assure the authenticity of Amish practices and customs. Old Order Amish and New Order Amish may be portrayed in this work of fiction and may differ from some communities. Although the book may be set in a certain locality, the practices featured in the book may not necessarily reflect that particular district's beliefs or culture. This book is purely fictional and built around a fictional community, even though you may see similarities to real-life people, practices, and occurrences.

We, as *Englischers*, can learn a lot from the Plain People and their simple way of life. Their hard work, close-knit family life, and concern for others are to be applauded. As the Lord wills, may this special culture continue to be respected and remain so for many centuries to come, and may the light of God's salvation reach their hearts.

ONE

Janie frowned as she examined the store shelf she'd just stocked. She'd always been a stickler for neatness and organization, sometimes to a fault. She reached for the package of pancake mix to move it in line with the others, scrutinizing the Amish buggy emblazoned on the front.

A young boy rounded the corner, a fistful of honey sticks in his chubby hand. The little guy's plump cheeks seemed to glow as he proudly offered her one of his treasures.

Janie bent down and accepted his gift. "Oh, is this for me?" she spoke in Pennsylvania German.

The toddler prattled on in gibberish, causing a smile to tug at Janie's heart. What she wouldn't give to have a little one of her own. But that hadn't been *Der Herr's* will for her. She knew better than to entertain thoughts of what might have been – what could have been.

She forced her attention back to her duties, but not before realizing the boy had abandoned his honey sticks on the floor. Where was the boy's mother? She glanced down just before he reached for a bottom book on the shelf behind her, but it was too late. The books on top began to topple over so she instinctively shielded the little guy from injury, to her own regret. Not that she regretted protecting the little one—just the headache she'd surely endure for the remainder of the day.

The loud crash caused customers to look her way and an Amish man in his late twenties finally appeared to claim the boy.

"Bobby, *nee*!" The man shook his head and gathered up the honey sticks, sheepishly apologizing for his son's behavior. They soon disappeared around the same corner the little one had emerged from.

A few moments later, she waved goodbye to the little guy as he exited the store with one of his suspender straps securely in his father's grasp. She continued to watch as little Bobby, his siblings, and his father drove down the lane in their family buggy.

Bobby. Was it short for Robert? She couldn't remember if she'd ever known an Amish *bu* with that name. She liked it.

~

"It's beginning to look a lot like Christmas," Her father's bright blue eyes held joy as he sang the words to the song. *"Ain't so, dochder?"*

"*Jah*. We've been quite busy now that Thanksgiving has passed." Janie moved the feather duster between the toys on the shelf.

"Tourists." He pointed through the store window to a middle-aged couple that were happily entering a vehicle with their Amish-made treasures in hand. "The best kind of shoppers. They've got money to spend and are always looking for special Amish-themed items. Perhaps we should order some post cards and t-shirts."

Janie burst out laughing.

"What? What did I say?"

"T-shirts? Really, *Dat*?"

"Could be good for business. None of the other dry goods stores are selling them in these parts." He scratched his grey beard. "We're nearly out of your potholders and dolls again. If we sold other things, we'd still turn a profit, and you wouldn't have to work so hard."

"I don't mind, *Dat*. It keeps me busy."

After that comment, a silence fell over them and Janie knew what they were both thinking. She had to stay busy to keep her mind off of the fact that she was the only *alt maedel* in their community. But she'd already come to terms with the fact that she would never marry and have a family of her own. It had been difficult to accept at first, but she'd resigned herself to *Gott*'s will. After all, if He'd wanted her to have a husband and family of her own, He would have made that happen. But He didn't. And she was okay with that. *Gott* knew what was best and He had His reasons. Who was she to question?

"Janie?"

Had her father been speaking to her? "Yes, *Dat*?"

"You didn't hear a word I said, did you?"

She smiled and guessed. "T-shirts?"

"That's what I thought. No, we were beyond t-shirts. I mentioned the wholesale souvenir catalog that came in the mail today. I want you to go over it with me tonight and we can decide which new items to purchase. Does that sound *gut*?"

"*Jah*, sure. But do you think *Englischers* will still want to buy the stuff if it's not Amish made?"

"Some will, I suppose. They have all kinds of items. Key chains, pencils, dolls, stickers. They might even have an Amish tattoo." He chuckled. "I've heard tell that some of the 'Amish' dolls in Lancaster are actually made in China, if you can believe that."

"You're not going to buy dolls from China. Are you, *Dat*?" Janie gasped. "And a tattoo?"

"Calm down, *dochder*. I didn't say we will order them." He laughed. "Oh, wouldn't that get a rise out of Christi?"

"*Dat*!" Janie shook her head. "You should not egg on the deacon."

Her father had always been of the cantankerous sort. Come to think of it, he reminded her a lot of Widow Brenneman, a lady Janie helped out several times a week. Which reminded her... "*Dat*, I don't know if this evening will be a good time. I'm supposed to visit Widow Brenneman."

"*Ach*, that's right." He frowned. "Does that mean I'm on my own for supper?"

"I made fresh bread yesterday and there's some leftover soup in the refrigerator. All you'll have to do is heat it up."

"I suppose that will have to do."

Janie didn't miss her father's disappointed sigh. She knew that he'd hated dining alone ever since *Mamm* passed on to Glory. "You could join Widow Brenneman and me for supper."

"You don't think she'd mind?" His bushy eyebrow moved up a hair.

"Mind?" Janie laughed. "She'd be thrilled. You know she's taken a shine to you ever since you fixed her buggy wheel."

"*Ach*, that's just your imagination." He swatted the air in front of him. "No pretty young widow's gonna take a likin' to an old goat like me."

"*Dat*, she's only seven years younger than you. And you're not that old."

"She's too young."

Janie sighed. She sometimes wondered if her father purposely stayed unmarried because of her own singleness. Did he worry she might be lonely on her own?

Not that she wasn't lonely. She'd be lying to herself if she said that she didn't still long for what wasn't meant to be.

"You still thinkin' on that Yoder boy?" Her father's hand squeezed hers. "No good can come from it."

"I know." She forced down the lump clogging her throat. "He's not coming back. My only—" She ran to the stock room, not wanting her father to see her crying again. Elson had been dead for three years now, so why was it still so hard?

"Have you forgiven him?"

She wished her father hadn't followed her. It was so much easier to cry when she didn't have an audience. She soaked up a tear with her dress sleeve.

"I've tried."

"I know it may be wrong to say this, *dochder*, but I think you might just be better off without Elson Yoder."

"How can you say that, *Dat*? I loved him!"

"I know you did. But I wouldn't want to see you hurt. If he was drinking alcohol and driving an *Englischer's* vehicle, how do you know he wouldn't have put your life in danger too?"

"Elson didn't drink all the time, just once in a while." When he hung out with his *Englisch* friends, is what he'd told her. She knew it was just a phase and he'd outgrow it or give it up before he was baptized into the church. At least, that's what she'd hoped for. "He never would have put my life in danger. He loved me."

They'd already discussed marriage and planned a life together. But Elson, through his own foolishness, had succumbed to an early death. A preventable death. Fortunately, no one else had been in the vehicle with him when he veered off the road and into a telephone pole. He'd been pronounced dead at the scene, the EMS workers had said.

He'd been driving just a mile down the road from her home, most likely on his way to see her. When she and her father heard the sirens, they hitched up the buggy to go investigate. When they'd arrived at the scene, they hadn't known it was him. The victim's body had been covered with a white sheet.

Elson had already been identified by another community member, but Janie couldn't believe it. She insisted on seeing for herself. Afterward, she wished she hadn't.

She'd lost everything that day—her hopes and dreams and plans for her and Elson's future. It hurt to breathe.

The leaders maintained that it had been *Gott's* will, but she couldn't wrap her mind around that thought. Surely *Der Herr* didn't want Elson drinking alcohol and driving an *Englisch* vehicle. Surely *Der Herr* hadn't wanted Elson to leave this world at such a young age. *Nee*, she didn't agree with that concept. She did, however, acknowledge that *Der Herr* had allowed it to happen. And He hadn't stepped in and prevented it, either.

"Each man must make his own choices. Elson chose to put his own life in danger and jeopardize your future together," *Dat* had succinctly put it.

Unfortunately, she'd been left to deal with the consequences of his actions—a heart broken in two and a future devoid of a husband and *kinner*. Unless *Der Herr* had other plans for her, she couldn't see any way around those facts. And truthfully, she didn't know if she could ever open her heart to another man again.

TWO

"*Dat*, the delivery truck just pulled up!" Janie plunged her hands into the warm dishwater as she watched the driver exit his vehicle.

"I will meet him, *dochder*. You *chust* finish up those dishes so we can work on that puzzle."

She whistled and turned back to the task at hand.

Dat walked into the kitchen a moment later. "Well, wouldn't you know it. It's for you, Janie girl."

She frowned. "For me?"

He shrugged and held up the small box. "That's what is written here."

She nodded and turned back to her dishes.

Dat gasped. "Well? Aren't you going to open it?"

"You're worse than the *kinner*. Can't you wait till I'm done?"

"*Nee*. You know I never have been long on patience. *Kumm*, open it up."

Janie cast an exasperated look at her father. "Why don't you do it, since you're so anxious to see what's inside?"

"Oh, no. It has *your* name on it." He cut a coy look in her direction. "Got a secret beau you don't want your old *dat* to know about?"

She snorted. "Secret beau? *Nee, Dat*, there is no secret beau."

"You sure are taking your sweet time."

"*Dat*, the package has been in this house all of two minutes!"

He held out a pair of kitchen shears. "Here, use these."

She dried her dripping hands on a hand towel and took the box from his hands, examining it. "Hmm...Robert Zehr? Who is that? Does this address look familiar?"

"Not that I know of." *Dat* shrugged. "Maybe it's a secret admirer." He rubbed his hands together, his grin wide.

"A *secret* admirer would not put his name." She took the scissors and slid them under the tape. *Dat* helped open the box but allowed her to retrieve the contents it held. "A box of chocolates?"

Dat's grin widened. "I knew it! What does the card say?"

She read the brief note, which looked like it had been printed from a computer. "I think of you often. Wishing you a Merry Christmas!"

"See?" He pointed to the note. "He thinks of you. Often, it says." Her father, the hopeless matchmaker.

"*Dat*, I don't know. I think maybe it was sent by mistake?"

"It's addressed to you and the card has *your* name on it. It was definitely intended for you."

"But I don't know anyone named Robert Zehr."

"Sounds like an Amish name."

"*Jah*, it does." She held the open box out to him. "Would you like a chocolate?"

His eyes sparkled like a *kind* at Christmastime, and he rubbed his hands together. "I thought you'd never ask."

She reached for a chocolate covered toffee candy and popped it into her mouth. The buttery flavor exploded on her taste buds like vibrant display of Fourth of July fireworks. "Whoever you are, Robert, thank you."

"That's a *gut* idea, Janie girl!"

"What's a *gut* idea?" Oh, my. This was the most delicious chocolate she'd ever indulged in.

"You can send him a Thank-You card."

"But I don't know where he lives."

"The address is right there, *ain't not*?"

"*Dat*, I think that is the address of the candy company, not the person who sent it."

"Oh. Well, I suppose you can go use one of them computers at the library to find his address."

"You want me to cyber stalk him? Really?"

"Cyber...what?"

"Nothing. It's a term that Elson's *Englisch* friends used when talking about looking up people online."

"I don't know if you spending time with all those *Englischers* was such a *gut* idea. Now you know all these fancy words and I have no idea what you're even saying. It's almost like you're speaking a different language."

"Oh, *Dat*. Don't be such a drama king."

"A *what*? See? That's exactly what I mean."

"You're overreacting. I don't have a secret language. *Or* a secret beau. Chances are, this Robert person is some old bachelor. Maybe I should think twice about sending him a card. If he reads it the wrong way, we could have some sicko on our doorstep."

"Now who's the one overreacting?"

26

"Point taken. Okay, I'll look him up," she acquiesced.

"*Wunderbaar*! We better start growing the celery."

Janie couldn't help laughing out loud. "*Dat*, that was *your* wedding in Lancaster, Pennsylvania. They don't grow celery for weddings here."

"Well, they should. I loved that dish."

"Besides, *nobody* is getting married."

"We'll see about that." He chuckled.

"*Ach, Dat*!"

~

Janie typed in Robert's name just as the librarian suggested. While she'd heard about cyber stalking, she'd never actually done it herself.

Hmm. No one with the name Robert Zehr?

Well, good. Because this was a ridiculous notion anyhow. But she felt bad not even acknowledging the gift.

She looked at the envelope, shrugged, and typed in the address just out of curiosity. Instead of the candy shop she'd expected to appear before her eyes, the address was indeed attached to the name Robert Zehr.

So, she had her answer. She'd write out a proper note of gratitude, then send it off tomorrow. Her due diligence complete.

THREE

Rob yawned, then guzzled down the last of his coffee. His dog Rosco sat up, wagging his tail excitedly, then placed his spotted paw on Robert's shin.

"Just a minute, boy. I still need to finish my toast."

Rosco turned his head to the side and whined.

"No, you're not getting toast. Don't you like your dog food?"

Rosco whined again, then became distracted by the sound of the mail dropping into the box near the door. He rushed to the box, his tail wagging furiously, and waited patiently for Rob to gather his letters. It had become a daily ritual.

"What'd we get today, boy? More Christmas cards?" He opened up the metal box and reached inside. He stared down at the contents. "Bill. Christmas card from Mom and Dad. Hmm...what's this one?"

Rosco tilted his head.

"It looks too small to be a Christmas card."

Rosco nudged his hand with his wet nose.

"I'll open it, I'll open it. Just wait a minute." Rob chuckled. "You just want to go on that run with me, don't you? Okay, I'll try to hurry."

Rob moved to his desk and pulled out his letter opener. He glanced down at the three envelopes. Curiosity got the best of him, and he opened the small envelope first.

Thank you, the card boasted on the front along with a beautiful country scene. He opened it to read what was inside.

Greetings, Robert.

I'd like to say thank you for the chocolates you sent. I can't remember if we've ever met before or not. Your name does not sound familiar to me.

I don't know why you sent me chocolates, but it was a thoughtful thing to do, so I wanted to say thank you.

Sincerely,

Janie Mishler

P.S. Your name sounds Amish. Maybe we've met at a wedding?

Rob stared wide-eyed at the note in his hand, then finally placed it on his desk with a chuckle.

"Rosco, I have *no* idea who this is. And I didn't send anyone chocolates." He shook his head. "Strange."

No, the last time he'd purchased chocolate for someone had been... Wow, had it been five years already since Cynthia dumped him for Alvin Lengacher?

He sighed.

He was *not* going there again. No, he'd already spent way too much time lamenting Cynthia's departure. He wouldn't waste another minute on someone who couldn't care a rip about him.

As a matter of fact, he shouldn't think of Cynthia at all. According to his mother, she and Alvin had recently welcomed their third child.

He'd mulled their situation over in his mind so many times. What had he done wrong? What was it about him that repelled Cynthia? Why had she chosen Alvin Lengacher over him? What qualities had Alvin possessed that he hadn't?

And there he went, thinking about her again. All because of a card that he had nothing to do with. Who was this Janie Mishler, anyway?

Oh well, he would write back and tell her there must have been a mistake. Because he didn't plan to *ever* buy a woman chocolates again.

Rosco pawed his leg again.

"Alright, let's go for our run, boy!" His reply would have to wait.

~

Janie smiled as she read the return name and address on the envelope she held. Rob Zehr. *Robert?* She hadn't expected him to write back. Did people usually reply to Thank-You notes? Yet, she did mention his name sounding Amish.

What would he say to her?

She opened the letter the moment she stepped into her bedroom.

Dear Janie,

There must have been some mistake. I haven't sent chocolates to anyone.

To answer your question, no, I am not Amish. Although, I used to be. I left during my rumspringa to pursue an education in aviation. That was about five years ago. I have my private pilot's license now and I love to fly. Probably sounds funny to you for an ex-Amishman to be flying up in the sky. Unless your district is much more progressive (faster) than mine was.

Anyway, thanks for sending the Thank-You. I don't get too much mail other than bills, so an extra piece of personal mail is nice. I guess you have a mystery to solve now. That's weird you thought they were from me. I wonder how that could have happened.

And no, I don't believe we have met before. I've known Mishlers—as a matter of fact, I'm related to some—but don't recall a Janie Mishler. Who are your parents? Or, is that your married name? If it is, I imagine your husband might be curious why you are receiving chocolates from another man. Well, he can rest assured that I did not send them.

Sincerely,

Rob Z.

Janie couldn't seem to erase the smile off her face, even though it had been two hours since she'd read the letter. He flew airplanes? How exciting his life must be! She'd always wondered what it would be like to soar way above the world.

She determined to write him back before bed tonight. She'd send the letter off tomorrow. She couldn't wait to learn more about Robert—*nee*, Rob Zehr.

Greetings, Rob.

I hope it's okay if I call you Rob. If not, I don't mind calling you Robert. They are both nice names.

Anyhow, I don't even know where to begin to solve this mystery. Maybe some mysteries just aren't meant to be solved. I feel bad that Dad and I ate all the chocolates if they were supposed to be for someone else. Oh, no. What if they were supposed to be for you and that's why your name was on it? If that's the case, I'm sorry. They were really good.

I can't believe it that you fly airplanes. Should I wave next time I see one up in the sky? Or can you even see from way up there? It must be real exciting! I can only imagine what it's like.

Our district does permit air travel for certain occasions. I guess we are pretty fast compared to some.

Now, to find out who sent those chocolates and who they were meant for.

Thank you for writing back.

Sincerely,

Janie M.

P.S. Mishler is my father's name. And, no, I am not married.

Tomorrow her letter would send off. She could only hope that he'd respond again.

FOUR

Rob tossed his truck keys on the entry table as he walked through the front door. He'd forgotten his logbook today—something he never did. He'd been meticulous in the past about logging his flight hours as they occurred.

But his mind had been on something else today. Not a good thing when you're flying the friendly skies. His head had definitely been in the clouds, but not the way it should have been.

It had been the last line of Janie's letter that caused his mind to go haywire. *No, I am not married.* Why did that even matter to him? Maybe it was because he sensed a connection between them. Or that she'd said he had a nice name. Or that she was actually interested in what he did for a living. No, not just interested but excited about it.

Janie's reaction had been so different from Cynthia's when he'd mentioned his interest in flying to her. Cynthia had rolled her eyes, practically ripping the joy from his dream. Taken the wind from his sails. He'd never mentioned his dream to her again, nearly abandoned it all together. He'd been ready to give it up for her and settle down and join the church, if she didn't want to join him in the *Englisch* world. Instead, she'd fallen for Alvin Lengacher.

For the first time, it dawned on him that maybe Cynthia was not who God had planned for him. He'd thought she was and that he'd done something to blow his chances with her. But maybe God had a different plan for him all along. Maybe...no, he wouldn't allow his mind to go that direction. He'd never even met Janie Mishler face-to-face. For all he knew, she could be an elderly woman.

But...would an elderly woman show that much enthusiasm for flying? Would an elderly woman say that she and her *father* had eaten all the chocolates? No. Not to his thinking, anyway.

Janie Mishler had to be about his age or younger, he guessed, from the tone in her letters. He knew one thing. If he didn't find out more about Janie Mishler, his head would never descend from the clouds. Unless it was a crash landing.

~

"Another letter for you, *dochder*. From Rob." *Dat's* head tilted in her direction. "Is there something you're not telling me?"

"*Nee, Dat*. You know everything I do." She held out her hand for the letter.

"How many letters does this make now?" He held the envelope, purposely taking his sweet time. As though every second without knowing the words Rob penned wasn't pure torture.

"It's only the second one." She snatched the letter from his hand. "And stop looking at me like that. He flies airplanes. He's likely your age."

"Then why are you so eager for his words?" *Dat* challenged.

"I don't know. It's a mystery. And mysteries are exciting, ain't not?"

"I suppose."

She pointed at him. "Oh, don't even act that way. I know good and well that you are just as curious as I am."

"Just waiting for the word. You know, celery takes time to grow."

Janie burst out laughing. "*Dat*, you don't give up, do you? I am not marrying Rob Zehr. He's way too old for me."

"You don't know that."

"He's not even Amish, *Dat*! And if he flies airplanes, he will never be Amish again."

He rubbed his hands together and eyed the letter. "Are you done with your yacking yet?"

"Next time, I'm going to ask how old he is just to get those ridiculous notions out of your head."

"You do that." His lips curved into a grin. "Now open that letter."

She slipped her letter opener under the envelope's flap and pulled out the single page of stationary.

"Nice paper." Her father commented. "Not just from a notebook this time. That says something."

Janie laughed and shook her head. "What does it say, *Dat*?"

"He put some thought into it."

Her eyes moved to the words on the page.

Hello, Janie.

Since we're getting to know one another, I figure I should probably tell you a little about myself.

I'm twenty-seven. I live with my dog, Rosco. You already know that I pilot airplanes. I'm actually an instructor and teach others to fly as well. Sometimes people pay me to give them rides. It's a pretty cool job. I enjoy what I do.

You said you weren't married, so does that mean you work outside the home? If so, what kind of job do you have? How old are you, if you don't mind my asking?

As far as the mystery goes, I'll have to put my thinking cap on. Maybe the two of us can solve this thing together.

If you and your father ever find yourselves in the area, look me up. I love to show people around the friendly skies, especially if they've never been flying.

Looking forward to your next letter.

Your friend,

Rob Z.

Janie startled when *Dat* clapped his hands together behind her.

"I knew it! See, he's not too old. Perfect age, I'd say. Old enough to have outgrown his immaturity and know what he wants. Young enough to have fun with. That's important in a relationship."

"*Dat.*" Janie sighed. "He's a stranger."

"*Nee.* A friend. See? Says so right there."

"He's not Amish. How could you even encourage me in this?"

39

"I don't think those chocolates arrived by mistake. I think *Der Herr* delivered them exactly where He wanted them. I do not know what His plan is, but I'm sure He has one. Rob's a lost sheep, Janie. Perhaps *Der Herr* will use you to draw him back into the fold."

A giggle tripped from her lips. "If I didn't know any better, I'd think you've been reading those fancy Amish romance novels we sell in our store."

"Ah, so you've read them."

She shrugged. "One or two." She folded the letter and placed it in the letter box she kept in her room.

"Aren't you going to write him back?"

"I will. But I need to work on those inventory sheets."

"You let me work on the inventory."

"I've got it, *Dat*. Really. I'll send off a letter to Rob tomorrow."

FIVE

Disappointment creased Rob's brow as he set the mail on the kitchen table. "No letter today, Rosco." He scratched his dog's head.

Had his life really become this boring? When the thought of checking the mail was the highlight of his day? He really needed a life. He needed a friend. Someone, other than Rosco, to help fill his days.

He'd had a couple close friends when he'd been Amish, but once they'd begun their families, they were too occupied to do all the things they used to do together. Not that he blamed them. If he had a family of his own, he'd be the same way. Too enamored with his wife to think about much else.

But Cynthia had ripped that dream from him too.

He squeezed his eyes shut. "God? Is this all you have for me? Or is there something more? Because, while I enjoy flying, it doesn't fulfill my deepest longings."

I am enough for you.

Wow! Had that voice been audible?

"I'm sorry, God. I know. Yes, You are enough. But didn't You say that it is not good that man should be alone? You fashioned Eve for Adam."

No response.

"I trust You, Lord. Just, if You could give me contentment. I thought I was content before Janie's note arrived. But something about it stirred up this longing. I thought it was gone. I thought it was dead and buried. Please lead me, God."

~

The next day, her letter arrived, and he wasted no time tearing into it.

Greetings, Rob!

You wanted to know about me, so here it goes.

I am twenty-five years old. It's just me and my father at home. I have a sister and two brothers, which all have families of their own.

My father and I run Mishler's Dry Goods. I enjoy spending my days with Dat at the store. I get to meet interesting people all the time.

I can't speak for my father, but I'd love to go flying sometime.

Where do you think we should start with this mystery? I can't think of the next step. Other than your name and mine, I have no other clues.

Tell Rosco hello.

Your friend,

Janie

Short and sweet.

"Mishler's Dry Goods?" he said aloud. He rubbed Rosco's head. "I've been there before, Rosco. I know exactly where it is."

The dog whined.

"Yeah, she said to tell you hello, too. And get this, Rosco. She's twenty-five. And single."

Rosco stared at him.

"Well, it's worth a shot, right? It's not like it would hurt to meet her in person. Looks aren't everything. Besides, just cause she's single doesn't mean she's not attractive. I'm attractive, aren't I? And I'm single."

Rosco covered his eyes with his paw.

"What? Cynthia found me attractive. No, I wouldn't be on the cover of any magazines or anything. And I don't expect Janie to be either. She's nice. That should be enough."

Rosco licked his hand.

"Was that an affirmation? Do you think I should meet her?"

Rosco's head tilted to the side.

"Oh, *you* want to meet her too? I planned to fly over there, Rosco. You don't like flying, remember? You're not The Red Baron."

His canine companion placed a paw on Rob's leg.

"Alright, I'll take the truck. But Mishler's Dry Goods is at least an hour away. You'll have to ride up front with me. It's too cold now for you to ride in back."

Rosco sat up and panted.

"What? You want to go *now*?" Rob shrugged. "Why not? I don't have any clients scheduled today. And neither one of us is going to get anything accomplished until we see this thing through."

He was having a conversation with his dog. Yeah, he needed a life.

SIX

Two hours later, Rob pulled into the small parking area of Mishler's Dry Goods. He glanced down at his choice of clothing—dark jeans and a green Henley. Cynthia had said green brought out the color of his eyes, which were hazel but reflected whichever shade of green he wore.

"Time to do this, Rosco. How do I look?"

The dog ignored him and stared over the dashboard, looking out the windshield with anticipation, his tongue dangling over his bottom lip.

"I'll have to come for you later. You be good."

Rosco eyed him, then sat up straight on the seat.

"Good boy. I'll bring her out to meet you in a while, okay?" He briefly examined his teeth and hair in his visor mirror. "Wish me luck."

He approached the store with a confidence he hoped to eventually feel. Really, Janie didn't even know he was coming. If he lost his nerve, he could simply buy something, turn around and walk out. No harm. No foul. She'd have no idea it was him. And Rosco would forgive him if he didn't get to meet her.

The moment the door swung open, the freshly made soft pretzels beckoned his taste buds. He'd know that smell anywhere. Instantly, he was a little Amish boy sitting at his *grossmammi's* table on Saturday morning. Salt hitting his tongue, warm dough melting in his mouth.

"May I help you, sir?"

His attention shot to an older man. Was this Janie's father? "Uh, yes. You sell soft pretzels?"

"I believe my daughter just pulled some from the oven. Should be hot and fresh!" His eyes twinkled.

He couldn't hide his smile if he tried. He liked this man already. "Perfect."

Rob approached the counter near the back of the store and waited in line until the customer in front of him had been helped. He couldn't see the woman's face as she prepared the customer's items.

Then she glanced up. Kind eyes and a friendly smile met him. Janie Mishler wasn't the most beautiful woman he'd ever seen, but she was certainly pretty in her own right. He could barely tear his gaze away from her attractive smile.

Once the customer left, her gaze rested on his, causing his heart to somersault. "May I help you?"

He blinked, breaking the momentary spell. "Uh, yeah. I'd like three pretzels."

"Three? Okay." Her grin remained in place as she took a pair of tongs and reached into the glass warming case.

"You wouldn't happen to have an airtight container to put one of those in, would you? I'm afraid my dog would sniff out my extra pretzel and eat it before we got home."

"Your dog?" She nodded. "Um, we sell some plastic containers. Do you think that would work? They're over in aisle three."

He turned in the direction she'd gestured.

"There are no customers after you. I can show you where to find them."

"Thank you. I appreciate that." He blew out his breath as he followed her to aisle three. How was he going to reveal himself to her?

"They're right here." She gestured to the second-to-bottom shelf, then picked up a container. "This one should be about the right size. But you probably don't want to use it until after it's washed. They usually have chemicals in them."

"Oh." He frowned.

"I can take it in the back and wash it for you. It's no problem."

He smiled. Yeah, she was just as sweet as he'd imagined. "That's kind of you. I appreciate that."

"It's no problem." She repeated, quickly disappearing around the counter, then through a set of double doors.

~

Janie quickly washed the container with soap and water, eager to hand it back to the handsome *Englisch* customer. It wasn't often young men entered the store alone. Perhaps the pretzel sign out front had lured him in. She couldn't fault him for being drawn to soft pretzels, it was one of her favorite snacks. As a matter of fact, after this man exited the store, she planned to indulge in one herself.

"Anything else?" She handed back the clean container.

"Uh, yeah, actually. Let me get one more."

"Four all together, then?"

"That's right. I know Rosco is going to want one of these for himself."

Rosco? She tilted her head, pressing her lips together. She'd heard that name before. *Wait.*

48

He smiled and extended his hand toward her. "I'm Rob Zehr."

This was Rob Zehr? *Oh my*. Had her face caught fire? "The chocolate guy." She finally recovered.

"That's me. Although I'm usually the airplane guy." He chuckled. "And technically, I *didn't* send the chocolates so I probably shouldn't get credit for it."

"Right. The mystery."

He handed over the money for the pretzels and the container. "I bought one of these for you." He held up the bag of pretzels.

"For me?" She couldn't suppress her smile.

"I hope you'll join me? Outside? If you can get away." He turned and looked behind him. There were no more customers in the store.

"Sure. I'll just...*kumm*, my father will be glad to meet you." She rounded the counter, placing her apron on a wall hook.

"And Rosco's waiting to meet you." His boyish grin stole her breath away. "He's in the truck. Probably wondering what's taking me so long."

"Well, I'm excited to meet him too." She led the way to the front counter where her father held a box cutter in his hand.

49

"Will you get the keys and lock up?" *Dat* hadn't glanced up from his task at hand. He patted the box. "This is our catalog order, I'm sure. Just in time for Christmas."

"*Dat*, I—"

He finally looked up. "*Ach*, I didn't realize we still had a customer."

"*Dat*, this is Rob Zehr. The one who *didn't* send the chocolates."

"Oh." *Dat's* eyes widened, then briefly flickered to Janie. "*Gut. Gut* to meet you, Rob." He stood and shook their visitor's hand.

"You too, Mr. Mishler."

"Joash." *Dat's* smile glistened.

"Nice to meet you, Joash."

"So, what brings you out this way?"

"Uh, Janie, actually." He shrugged. "When I read in her letter that you owned Mishler's Dry Goods, I remembered stopping by before. I thought it would be nice to meet in person. And Rosco wanted to go for a drive."

"Rosco?"

"My dog. He's waiting in the truck. He's probably pretty anxious to get out right about now."

"We're going to step outside, *Dat*." She could read his expression without him saying a word. He would likely call in an order for celery seeds the moment they stepped out the door.

"You two take all the time you need. I've got plenty to do here." He pointed to the large box in front of him. *Dat's* souvenirs. No doubt, he was dying to add them to their inventory.

Rob nodded. "Thank you, Joash. It was nice meeting you."

"You're not leaving yet, are you?" *Dat* frowned. "You've come all this way. Might as well stay for supper. Right, Janie?"

"*Ach, jah*. Of course, if you want to."

Rob studied her pensively. "You're sure?"

She nodded with a smile. "Absolutely."

"Yeah, okay then." A smile stretched across his lips. "It looks like Rosco and I are staying for dinner."

He moved to the truck and opened the door. "Hey, buddy. Janie's here. You wanna come meet her?"

The dog sat on the seat, his tail waving back and forth like the pendulums on the clocks they sold in the store.

"Come on!" Rob clapped, which resulted in Rosco leaping from the vehicle. "Good boy."

He chuckled and turned to her. "As you can see, Rosco's ecstatic."

"Hello, Rosco. Nice to meet you." She knelt down and scratched him behind the ears.

"He loves that. You'll be his new best friend." He glanced around and pointed to a bench they kept in the yard. The store was an extension of their home. "Let's sit and enjoy our pretzels?"

She'd nearly forgotten their treat. She nodded. "Rosco seems to have found a friend in the neighbor's dog."

"Rosco, be nice. And don't stray too far. I don't want to have to go searching for you." Rob turned to her. "Better that he be off with another dog than begging for our pretzels, I guess."

He sat on the bench and she eased down beside him. He opened the bag and offered her one of his savory snacks.

"*Denki.*" She smiled in delight as she pulled the still-warm pretzel from the bag. "One of my favorite things."

He reached into the bag and pulled off a steaming section of dough, then popped it into his mouth. "Mine too. Must be my lucky day."

She lifted her face to capture the warmth of the waning sunshine. "It's been a nice day."

"It has." He nodded, then seemed to notice her attire. "Are you cold?"

"*Ach*, there's just a little chill in the air."

"Here, take my jacket."

Before she could protest, he'd removed his jacket and placed it around her shoulders. She'd only ever worn one other man's jacket--Elson's. There was just something about wearing a man's coat. A sign of security, of belonging. It was almost like a hug. Was she reading too much into Rob's kind gesture? Probably.

She fought with her senses to resist inhaling the masculine scent of the cologne on his jacket. Was she dreaming this all up?

"*Denki*," she managed to squeak out.

"Tell me about yourself, Janie."

She smiled. "What do you want to know?"

"Do you...have a boyfriend? Anybody courting you?"

Her cheeks warmed. "*Ach*, uh, no."

"Why? How?" He chuckled. "Sorry if I'm being nosy. I'm just thinking that some lucky Amish man would have snatched you up by now. You're twenty-five, right?"

"I, um, *had* a boyfriend. Elson Yoder. He died in a car accident about three years ago. We...we'd planned on getting married before..."

"Oh." He frowned. He moved his hand toward hers, then seemed to think better of it and pulled back. "I'm so sorry."

She wanted to change the subject. She didn't want to have thoughts of Elson when this handsome man was beside her. "And what about you? Girlfriend?"

"Nope. Not in quite a while."

"How come you left the Amish?" She tugged in her bottom lip. "Maybe I shouldn't ask."

"No, it's fine. I don't mind. Well, long story short, my girlfriend of a year and a half dumped me for another guy. I always had a dream of flying and it was something she didn't support. She married the guy and I became a pilot." He shrugged. "I guess it worked out for both of us."

If only he was still Amish.

"Do you miss your family?"

"Sure. But I can see them anytime. I'm not in the *Bann* or anything."

"That's *gut*."

"We occasionally write letters back and forth. My mom wishes I lived closer. I was never baptized into the Amish church. I guess they worry about that, but I'm fine. I mean, I've trusted in the Lord for my salvation. And from what I read in the Bible, one doesn't have to be Amish to be saved or get to Heaven."

"*Nee*, just believing in Jesus."

"That's right." He finished off his pretzel, then turned to her. "Do you...uh, are you *interested* in a relationship?"

"What do you mean? Like, in general?"

"No." He grinned and shook his head. "I meant...with me. I know it might sound a little forward. But I feel like we already know each other because of our letters."

Now she was certain her cheeks were ablaze. Was she interested? *Ach*, definitely! But could she act on it? No, she could not.

"I am baptized." He would understand without her explaining.

"I figured as much." He nodded. "And I'm not. Which, according to the Amish church, makes us unequally yoked."

"*Jah*." Unfortunately. *If only...*

"According to God, though, if we've both trusted Christ, we're not unequally yoked," he reasoned.

"You know I'm required to follow the *Ordnung*." She frowned.

"Yeah. I was afraid you'd say that." He shook his head and sighed. She sensed his disappointment. "I probably shouldn't even have asked. But I know I'd regret it if I didn't. So, just friends, then?"

She smiled, but regret tore at her heart. "*Jah*, friends."

"Okay, now that we got that out of the way..." He clapped his hands and rubbed them together. "Let's solve a mystery?"

She didn't know what exactly it was about Rob Zehr, but she *really* liked this man. He seemed kind, thoughtful, and near perfect as far as suitors went. Why couldn't he be Amish? "I don't know where to start."

"The candy company?"

"I've thought of that. It seems like it came from an online store, though, and not the actual candy company."

"Hmm." He rubbed the back of his neck, which accentuated his bicep. She tried not to notice the pull of his shirt against his muscular frame. "Do you still have the package they came in?"

"*Nee*. I just kept the part with your name. I didn't see anything else that would identify a different sender."

"We could contact the store, tell them who it was sent to, and ask who the sender was."

"But wouldn't they say it was from you? Since that's how they sent it?"

He shrugged. "We could ask how it was paid for. If it was online, they probably used a credit card. I don't think they'd have any issues with giving us a name, right?"

"I guess it wouldn't hurt to ask." She shrugged. A breeze kicked up, causing her to shiver. "I should probably get supper ready."

"Right. And I should check on Rosco." They both stood from the bench.

"Thank you for the pretzel." She removed his jacket from her shoulders and reluctantly handed it back to him. She wished she could keep it close indefinitely.

"My pleasure." He glanced about the yard. "Is there somewhere you'd prefer I keep Rosco?"

"You could put him in the barn. It will at least keep him from the chilly wind."

"Do you have mouse catchers in there? Because he loves to chase cats." He winked.

"They'll just hide up in the loft."

"Okay. I'll see you inside in a little bit. I might stop in and say hello to your father again."

"He'd like that." With a content sigh, she meandered into the house.

Rob Zehr would be taking supper with them tonight. She couldn't wait to see what other surprises this day would hold.

SEVEN

"You fly airplanes, eh?" Joash's voice greeted Rob as he stepped back into the store. "Let me lock that behind you."

"Yep. I love soaring above the clouds."

"More than the love of a woman?"

Rob coughed. Had he just heard this man correctly? "Well..." He shrugged. "I can't say I've ever thought of it that way. Never considered it."

"Because, if you want Janie, you may have to choose."

"What makes you think—"

"You don't fool me, boy. I saw the way you were looking at *mei dochder*."

Was he *that* obvious? "I just...I came here because I wanted to meet her. Now that I have, I know my first instincts were correct. Janie is sweet and kind and will make a good friend. But I am not Amish anymore. I don't know if I'll ever be."

"Then I suggest you cut ties now. No sense in leading her on."

"We've already agreed that our relationship cannot go beyond friendship."

"And you're confident you can *keep* it at that?" Joash crossed his arms over his chest and cast a critical eye in Rob's direction. "My *dochder* has had her heart broken once before. I'm afraid she still hasn't recovered. Her heart has been closed up. But I can see her opening her heart again. To you."

"I would never break her heart."

"You say that with confidence."

"Let's just say that I've had a little experience in that department—on the receiving end. I wouldn't wish it on anyone."

"And how do you plan to avoid it?" His bushy gray brow quirked half an inch.

He attempted to swallow the lump lodged in his throat. This was a conversation he had *not* been anticipating nor was he prepared for. Had somebody turned up the furnace? "I don't know if I'm prepared to answer that question, honestly."

"Have you considered returning to the Amish? Settling down?"

"I have not. But last I checked, being a pilot was not exactly an approved Amish occupation."

"There was a time when working in an RV factory wasn't an approved Amish occupation, either. There was a time riding a bicycle was not allowed."

"What are you saying?"

"If that is all that is preventing you from returning to your Amish roots, why not speak with the leaders? Much has changed in recent years."

"Not in the district I'm from."

"I think you will find it different here."

"Do you think I should go before the leaders?"

"I'd say it wouldn't hurt. What have you got to lose?"

"Nothing, I guess." He frowned. No matter how liberal this Indiana district was, he was quite certain he'd be forced to resign before they'd accept him into their fold.

But Joash was right. It didn't hurt to speak with the leaders.

"I'll get you the number of our bishop."

"I'd appreciate that."

"And if you could keep this between us, I'd be thankful. No need to get Janie's hopes up."

Rob nodded. "I understand."

~

Rob shut the door after coaxing Rosco into his truck, but he remained outside. He turned to Janie. "Thanks again for supper. I haven't had a meal that good in a long time."

"*Denki*."

"So, you ready to go flying with me?" He rubbed his hands together to release some of his excitement. He always felt this way about flying, but the thought of flying with Janie by his side was doubly thrilling.

"*Ach*, you're serious?" She shivered, although she wore a sweater.

He shouldn't have allowed her to follow him outside. He slipped off his jacket and insisted she wear it. He'd only be cold until he entered the truck.

"Oh, yeah." He remembered the first time he'd been up in the air. He'd never felt more invigorated in his life. Flying was second nature to him now.

"When?"

"When are you free?"

"*Ach*, see that's just the thing. I work every day except Sunday."

"Could you go on a non-church Sunday then?"

"I suppose. But...do you work on Sundays?"

He chuckled. "Trust me. Flying isn't work. It's no different than you driving your carriage on Sunday. My work is teaching others to fly."

"If you're sure?"

"I am."

"I'd need to talk to *Dat*, to make sure he's okay with it."

"Certainly. I can take him up too if he'd like." But honestly, he hoped it would be just the two of them.

"There's no meeting this Sunday."

"Perfect. Talk to your father and if he's okay with it, give me a call. I can pick you up early Sunday morning." A gust of wind picked up. "I'd better get going."

She began removing his jacket, but he protested.

"No. You'll need it for the walk back to the house. I'll be plenty warm in the truck. You can give it back on Sunday. I have another at home."

Holding his gaze, she nodded.

He reached up and lightly stroked her cheek with his thumb. *Ach*...he suddenly cleared his throat and dropped his hand.

"Well, goodbye." He leaned forward and offered a brief hug, yearning to keep her in his arms longer. As much as he was tempted to graze her cheek with a kiss, he wouldn't. Keeping his promise to Joash wasn't going to be easy.

He opened his truck door and slid into the driver's seat. "Thanks again."

She smiled and waved as he drove down the long country lane.

Sunday couldn't come soon enough.

~

Janie's lips curved up in contentment as she stepped back into the house. She buried her face into the jacket's collar and inhaled deeply, thankful to be enveloped in a physical reminder of Rob. She'd cherish those last moments and dream many dreams, no doubt, even if they agreed to only friendship.

"Don't get your hopes up too high. He's still *Englisch*."

Her eyelids popped open at her father's warning. She hadn't realized he'd been watching her. Had he seen them through the window, when his hand caressed her cheek and he'd held her close? Warmth suddenly crawled up her neck at the thought of *Dat* seeing her embrace a young man. "*Ach*. I know, *Dat*."

"I hear a 'but' in your tone." *Dat* dipped his head.

"He's very nice, ain't not?"

"He seems like a *gut Englisch* boy." He reminded again, emphasizing the word *Englisch*.

And, of course, he was *but* he had Amish roots. "Do you mind if I go flying with him on Sunday?"

Dat's head shot up like a rocket. "Sunday? Flying on *Der Herr's* day?"

"He said it's no different than riding in a buggy on Sunday. Just another form of transportation."

"Transportation is to take one somewhere for a specific purpose. I'm not sure flying around for pleasure qualifies."

Her spirits plummeted. She was hoping *Dat* would approve.

"But the decision is up to you, *maedel*."

She sighed in relief. "He invited you to come along too, if you'd like."

Dat chuckled. "I think I'll keep my feet firmly planted on the ground."

"He said it's safer than riding in a buggy."

"Is that so?" He scratched his hoary beard. "*Nee*, it's not for me, *dochder*."

Nevertheless, she'd be counting the minutes until tomorrow when she'd call Rob to let him know she'd go with him.

Just the two of them. Together for hours. Riding in his truck or way up in the sky.

It sounded heavenly.

EIGHT

Rob pulled out his cell phone, prior to slipping into bed. Just in case Janie had called already, he didn't want to miss it. But instead of a call from Janie, the number from his parents' phone shanty showed on his missed calls. There was no sense calling back tonight. His folks would have turned in over an hour ago.

He tapped to play the message they'd left.

"Hello, Robert. It's *Mamm*. Could you come home? Your *Dat* has had a stroke..."

Rob wasn't sure if he even comprehended the remainder of the message. His father had a stroke? But his dad had always seemed strong as an ox. How could he have suffered a stroke?

"God, please let *Dat* be okay." Dread filled him as he hastily dressed back into his clothes. If he left soon, he'd be able to make it to the landing strip in Pennsylvania in less than two hours. He wasn't terribly tired, but he'd take along a cup of licorice root tea just in case. *Mamm* had always said it was healthier than coffee and worked just as well at keeping one alert, if not better.

Hopefully, she had a remedy for *Dat* as well.

For what it was worth, he called the phone shanty and left a message. If anyone listened to it, hopefully he'd have a ride to his parents' home from the airport. If not, he'd have to figure something else out when he arrived.

~

The weather had been perfect for his flight. Fortunately, a vehicle awaited him just outside the entrance gate. Good, someone had listened to the message he'd left.

He approached the car but...

He blinked. Was Cynthia behind the wheel? *Nee*, his eyes must be playing tricks on him.

The driver's side door opened, and Cynthia nearly bulldozed over him when she catapulted herself into his arms.

"Robert! I've missed you so much."

He pried her arms from his neck, holding her at arm's length. He surveyed her clothing. "You're...*Englisch*?"

She nodded. "I am. I'll explain it all to you on our drive back." She opened the car door and slid into the driver's seat.

He lowered himself onto the tiny seat, then glanced in her direction. His brow furrowed in confusion. "But...what about...is your husband...?"

"We're practically divorced." She didn't seem to be upset about that fact.

He frowned and unintentionally slammed the door shut. He was used to his sturdy pickup, not the tiny piece of tin Cynthia drove. "Why?"

She maneuvered the vehicle out onto the road, heading toward his childhood home. He and Cynthia had not only been sweethearts, they'd been neighbors growing up. "Alvin turned abusive."

"*Ach...*"

With a shaky hand she wiped away a tear. "We tried to get counseling. The leaders insisted we stay married, but I can't live like that, you know?"

"I'm sorry to hear that." He reached over and lightly touched her shoulder, offering support. "So you became *Englisch*?"

She shrugged. "I figured either way I'd be shunned."

"What about the *kinner*?"

"I have them most of the time now, due to a court ruling. The leaders weren't happy about that either." She sucked in a breath. "Oh, Robert! I never should have left you for him. I was so foolish."

Anger burned in his stomach and he bit back an uncharitable retort. "No, you shouldn't have."

"Can we...is there a way we can get back what we had?" Her hopeful look threatened to break down his defenses.

He wasn't prepared for this. For these feelings to come rushing back. He had another chance to be with Cynthia? What he wouldn't have given to hear those words years ago. But *now*?

No, it was too late. He'd moved on. He shook his head, then turned his gaze to the scenery. He could only make out a few things in the darkness.

"There's someone else, isn't there?"

He couldn't help the slight smile that tugged at his lips. "Yes."

"Are you married?"

"No." He didn't miss her smirk at his answer. If she thought he'd come crawling back to her, she was wrong.

"What's her name?"

"Janie. Janie Mishler."

"Is she pretty?"

He closed his eyes, remembering her heart-stopping smile. "Very."

"Figures." She hit the steering wheel. "I was hoping you'd take me up." She pointed to the roof of the car.

He stared at her. "You mean up in the air?"

"Yeah."

"But I thought—"

"The only reason I protested before was because we were Amish and I didn't want you to jump the fence."

"I'm here to see my family. The only flying I'll likely be doing is a trip back to Indiana."

"I know." She sighed. "I'm back at home. At my folks' place."

Next door. *Great.*

"They took the kids and me in. At least we have a place to stay." She rambled on even though he kept silent. "The leaders didn't like that, so my folks are sort-of in the *Bann* now too."

He nodded absently, not really wanting to hear any more of Cynthia's sob story.

"Your family has always been kind to me and the kids. But, of course, they have to shun me when the leaders are around."

He pulled out his wallet when they arrived a hundred years later—at least it seemed like it listening to Cynthia drone on and on about her miserable life. "How much do I owe you for the ride?"

"Oh, no. It was my pleasure."

He thrust a twenty into her hand. "Treat the kids to something then."

"Thank you." Her eyes clouded again. "You always were sweet."

"Goodbye, Cynthia."

He hurried up the porch steps before she prattled on for another twenty minutes. The ride home in her car had been more taxing than his anxious flight over. He'd worried about his father, but at least then he'd had peace and quiet. Had Cynthia always talked so much? Or was it just that it bothered him now?

NINE

Rob yawned and stretched out on his parents' comfy couch. It had always been one of his favorite pieces of furniture, even though it was worn and old. This sofa was home.

Mom had left a note on the kitchen table informing him that she'd be staying with Dad up at the hospital tonight. She suggested he get some sleep and catch a ride to the hospital in the morning. He planned to do just that.

Pounding on the door startled him awake. He forced himself from the couch and slugged over to see what all the commotion was about.

Did he hear a baby crying? He yanked the door open, fighting to keep his eyelids pried open.

"I'm sorry. I woke you up, didn't I?" Cynthia bounced a screaming baby in her arms. "Is...is your mom here?"

He frowned and forced himself to fully awaken. "No. She's at the hospital with my dad."

Disappointment filled her features. "Oh, no. I was hoping she'd have something to calm the baby."

"What's wrong with him?"

"Her. I think she might have colic."

A gust of wind reminded him December blanketed the land. "Come in. It's too cold out there for a baby."

"I don't know what I'm going to do. She won't sleep and my dad was yelling to keep her quiet."

Pity overtook him when he noticed her tears surface. "I might know where she keeps some catnip and fennel tincture. Let me check."

Cynthia followed him into the kitchen, where he rummaged through his mother's cabinets. "Not here. I'll check the bedroom and bathroom."

His mother had always kept an herb bag in case she was called on to visit someone in need of her time-tested remedies. Some people called her a healer, but she'd always deflected the praise, asserting *Der Herr* was the only one who could heal. She just used the gifts He had provided in nature.

A moment later, he found the tincture. He returned to the living room, where Cynthia continued to jostle the wailing baby.

Her lips twisted. "She just threw up all over me."

"Why don't you run home and change? I can give the baby the tincture."

"Are you sure?"

He nodded. It had been quite a while since he'd held a baby. "It's no problem. But please don't be long."

He reached for the baby and quickly administered a dropperful of the tincture, per the instructions on the bottle.

"I'll be right back, then."

He watched Cynthia hurry out the door. As soon as she did, the little one began calming down. Quiet filled the room once again.

"There now," he soothed. "Is your tummy feeling better?"

He feathered a hand over the baby's soft hair. She couldn't have been more than four or five months old. The little one hiccupped and her large eyes began to droop.

"You're exhausted, aren't you? You poor thing. I know the feeling. I am too." He returned to the couch and propped his feet up on the coffee table. He yawned and placed the sleeping baby on his chest.

He held her secure with one hand and gently caressed her chunky arm with the other. A content sigh escaped his lips as the little one's breathing slowed.

What would it be like to have a little one of his own? Perhaps if he and Janie pursued a relationship, it wouldn't be too long before...

Whoa! He was getting the buggy way ahead of the horse. He hadn't even experienced the pleasure of kissing her. And it *would* be a pleasure, he had no doubts. But he didn't even know if he would be returning to the Amish. He was quite certain she wouldn't be jumping the fence for him. No, he couldn't see her leaving her father.

The door opened and Cynthia slipped back inside the house. She entered the living room and approached the sofa.

"She's out," he whispered.

"How did you do it?" Cynthia whispered back.

"I think the tincture along with what she expelled on you helped to calm her stomach. Is she allergic to something she ate, do you think?"

"Maybe she can't tolerate her formula."

"You should talk to my mom. She'd be able to give you advice. I think I remember her recommending diluted goat's milk to someone in the past. Have you tried that?"

She sunk down next to him on the sofa. "*Nee*, but I will if she thinks it can help Becky."

"So that's her name?" He spoke softly, stroking the baby's soft hair.

"*Jah*. Becky Bear is what her daddy calls her."

Rob frowned. "It's too bad he won't be around to help your raise your children. I've always believed that children needed both a mother and a father."

She shrugged. "*Jah*, well, it doesn't always turn out that way."

"No, I guess it doesn't."

She gestured to the little one. "You would make a good father. I'm sure of it."

"You think so?"

She nodded. "If only..."

He hoped she wouldn't say the words. While he adored children, he had no intention of raising someone else's. Especially not ones that belonged to Cynthia and Alvin.

"Someday I hope to have my own." The little one sucked in a sharp breath, then a sweet smiled formed on her tiny lips. Was she dreaming?

"Their momma will be one lucky woman." Cynthia's fingers ever-so-softly trailed his forearm, causing him to flinch.

He scowled and shook his head in frustration, pulling his arm away. "*You* were the one who left *me*." He ground out the words.

"I can see now that was the worst mistake I ever made." Was she crying *again*? "Can we...is there any way we can try again?"

Seriously? "It's not something you can undo. You made your choice. You chose Alvin." He couldn't help the bitterness bundled up in his words. "And I've moved on."

"I should probably go." She sat forward.

"That's a good idea." He nodded curtly, then handed the sleeping baby to her.

"Goodbye, Robert." He didn't mistake the regret in her tone. "I hope you have a nice life."

TEN

Janie dialed Rob's cell phone and waited for what seemed like forever for him to pick up. In reality, it had only been three rings. But she was excited to tell him that she would go flying with him this Sunday.

"Hello?" a female voice answered.

Janie frowned, then glanced at the number. "I'm sorry, I think I dialed the wrong number." Her finger hovered over the End call prompt.

"Are you looking for Robert?"

"Rob, *jah*. Is...is this his phone?"

"It is," the woman said matter-of-factly.

"Oh. Is he there?"

Did she hear a giggle? "He's a little *busy* at the moment."

Why did this woman have Rob's phone? "Who is this?" Not that it was any of her business, but she had to know.

"Cynthia, his ex-girlfriend."

His ex-girlfriend? Didn't she live in another state? None of this made sense. "Where is he?"

"Uh...Pennsylvania."

Pennsylvania? "Why is he there?"

"I'm guessing he missed his home. And, you know, his *friends*."

There was something about this woman. She spoke differently, more sultry than a Plain woman would speak. "Are you...Amish?" Again, not her business. But she couldn't seem to stop her words.

"Not anymore. I'm *Englisch* now like Robert. And we...well... You know, I probably shouldn't be divulging his *personal* business."

Her gut twisted. Had they gotten back together? Is that why he was in Pennsylvania? Maybe getting involved with Rob wasn't such a good idea. "Could you tell him I called?" She swallowed the lump im her throat.

"Sure."

"This is Janie."

"Janie from...?"

"Janie Mishler. From Indiana."

"Indiana. And *who* do you work for?"

"I didn't call about work. I'm a friend of Rob's. Do you know when he's planning to return?"

"I think he may be staying with us through Christmas."

With us? "That long?"

"Look, I'd love to sit and chat with you all day, but I've got *other things* to do." The phone clicked off before she had a chance to say goodbye.

Janie stared at the phone. Rob hadn't said anything about going to Pennsylvania. Was he staying with his *Englisch* ex-girlfriend? It kind of sounded that way.

~

Rob walked down the hospital's corridor, chiding himself for leaving his cell phone at his folks' place. If Janie rang now, he'd miss her call. He'd been looking forward to hearing her voice, picturing her smile, even if it was over the phone. Too bad she hadn't called last night.

Thinking of last night... What a mess Cynthia had managed to make of her life. No, he realized it hadn't been all her fault. What had she meant by Alvin turned abusive? Did she mean that he physically laid hands on her? On the children? Because if she did...if he did... Hot resentment coursed through his veins. *No, Cynthia is no longer your concern!*

He felt torn between minding his own business and wanting to know the truth of the matter. But even if he did, it's not like he could *or would* do anything about it. She'd thrown him to the curb the moment she decided to pursue a relationship with Alvin. It was like she'd become bored with their relationship.

What if Janie finds me boring too? He grunted and shook off the self-deprecating thought. *I'm a pilot, for Pete's sake. How can* that *be boring?*

He buried his thoughts as he stepped into his father's hospital room. His heart plunged into his gut as he saw his once-strong, healthy father lying helplessly in a bed, and hooked up to machines.

Dad's head turned as Rob approached, his dull eyes sparking to life.

Rob quickened his steps until he'd enveloped his father in a hearty embrace. Tears pricked his eyes. "Dad. What happened?"

His father uttered something unintelligible, and Rob's eyes flew to his mother for the interpretation.

"I think he said you're finally home." She shrugged, then looked at Dad. "Am I correct?"

His father nodded slightly.

"For a little bit. I need to get back. I do plan on returning for Christmas, though."

Dad looked beyond where Rob stood. "*Fraa*?"

Rob was glad to be able to understand at least that. He chuckled. "No, no wife yet."

"Yet?" Interest piqued in his mother's tone.

"I recently met someone."

"Oh?"

"Yeah. I like her a lot. Her name is Janie."

His mother beamed. "Why don't you bring her home with you for Christmas?"

"Amish?" Dad's slurred voice drew his attention.

"Yes, Dad, she's Amish."

His mother clapped her hands together. "This is wonderful *gut*!"

He needed to stop his mother before she began planting celery.

"Mom. Really. We just met. We're barely getting to know each other. Nowhere near the marrying stage." He glanced down at his clothes. "And I'm still *Englisch*."

"By choice. That can change."

He chuckled. Janie's smile cut through his thoughts. "It could."

He needed to change the subject. And fast. "Um...Cynthia dropped by early this morning with a screaming baby. She was hoping you'd help with something for colic. I gave her the bottle of catnip and fennel. I hope that's okay."

"Where was it?" His mother frowned.

"I found it in your bathroom cabinet." He glanced at Dad and noticed his eyelids growing heavy.

Mom nodded. "That's my extra bottle. I'll need to make more. That seems to be a popular item these days with so many mothers choosing to use that store-bought formula."

He noted the disapproval in his mother's tone.

"Well, some have no choice, right?" Not that he wanted to get into a conversation about nursing mothers with his mom.

"There are many alternatives, but often they're not as convenient. But some *do* have a choice and choose not to for no good reason. I'll never understand that."

"You're talking about Cynthia?"

"*Ach*, that *maedel*!" *Mamm* shook her head. "Poor Alvin."

"Poor *Alvin*?" His voice screeched. "She said he was abusive."

"There are always two sides to every story, *sohn*. You shouldn't be so quick to believe without hearing both sides."

A rumble from his father's lips momentarily drew his attention. "What do you mean?"

"The *abuse* she's referring to is non-existent."

He jammed his arms across his chest. "Explain."

"The *boppli*. Alvin thought it belonged to someone else. Called her on it. He was right. She threatened to make up a story about him abusing her, if he took the matter to the leaders. He did."

He sighed. "So she did."

"Right. Needless to say, I'm glad it didn't work out between the two of you."

"Are you sure that is what happened and Alvin didn't make it up?"

"After the paternity test came back, I don't think *anyone* believed her. Plus, she kept changing her story. If the truth is told, the story stays the same."

His frown deepened. "What about her parents?"

"Henry believes Alvin. Barbara, on the other hand... I think she does too, but she feels obligated to defend her *dochder*."

A verse flashed through his mind. *He that answereth a matter before he heareth it, it is folly and shame unto him.*

Rob grunted. *God, forgive me for judging Alvin before hearing his side.*

"You're right. I guess God saved me from that mess." He shook his head, thankfulness filling his heart.

"That, He did."

He examined his father again as his chest rose and fell. "What are the doctors saying?"

"They don't have any real answers. Just want to push their pharmaceutical medicines, it seems. You know I worry about those."

He nodded. He did too. "I can search the internet to see what kind of side effects are reported, if you'll give me the names."

"*Denki. Jah*, I would feel better. Also, look up other treatments. Seems I heard about some oxygen-thing a while back."

"I'll do that. I can go by the library right now and use their computer. I left mine at home. I'd look it up on my phone, but I have a feeling I'll want to print out information for you."

Mom reached over and patted his hand. "You are *gut sohn*. Even if you are not choosing the Amish way."

86

He hitched a half smile. "I was raised right."

"Many are, but still choose their own devices."

"That's true." He nodded toward his father. "When will he be released?"

"They said tomorrow, if he's up and walking tonight."

"Already?"

"*Jah*. We don't have the money for them to keep him here if they're doing nothing to help. He can get better rest at home, which is the main thing he needs. He'll be happier there."

"What do you need from me? Besides research."

"If you could just stay long enough to get your *vatter* settled. I'm sure you have your work to get back to."

"I do." And Janie. Oh man, he couldn't wait to see her again.

ELEVEN

The research Rob had seen on Hyperbaric Oxygen Therapy had been promising. He couldn't wait to share what he'd learned with Mom.

As he pulled up to his folks' place, Cynthia waited in their driveway. *Wonderful.* He sighed. He was not looking forward to dealing with her again.

Nevertheless, he was grateful that she'd allowed him to use her car. He parked, then stepped out of the vehicle.

"Oh good, you're back."

"Yeah. Thanks for letting me use your car."

"Will you do me a quick favor, please?"

Great. "What is it?"

"Come with me to Alvin's? I'm afraid...I don't want to go by myself."

He planted his arms firmly across his chest and frowned. His first instinct was to say no. But something inside nudged him in the other direction. Perhaps he could get to the bottom of Cynthia's situation—and call her on the carpet.

"Sure." He found himself saying.

"Great. Let's go now? My *mamm* is watching the *kinner*."

He nodded, slipping back into the driver's seat. He'd always felt more comfortable being the one at the wheel. "Just tell me where to go."

Several moments later, they pulled up to a decent size farm. "Nice place."

Cynthia huffed and shook her head.

Alvin approached from the barn. The moment the vehicle rolled to a stop, Cynthia jumped out.

Rob took a deep breath and uttered, "I hope You know what You're doing, God, because I have no idea why I'm here."

He reluctantly stepped out of the vehicle. Cynthia flew to his side, but he took a step away.

He reached his hand to Alvin as he approached the vehicle.

Alvin scowled at his outstretched hand and glowered at Cynthia. "Let me guess. Another one of your *'boyfriends'*?"

A smirk rose on Cynthia's lips as she stepped near Rob again. "Maybe."

Alvin looked about ready to pound him into the ground.

Rob held up his hands. "No. I am *not*." He turned to his ex. "Cynthia, this foolishness needs to stop."

"What do you mean?" Did she just flutter her eyelashes?

"You two need to work out your problems," Rob insisted.

"You expect me to—" Cynthia's words were cut off.

"It's impossible. Besides, she has taken up with someone else. Has the *boppli* to prove it." Alvin's frown deepened.

"Are you not willing?" Rob looked to both of them.

"*Nee*. I'm tired of her games. And she obviously does not want me." Alvin shook his head. "She's been with other men. I do not need her in my life."

"He's been abusive," Cynthia claimed.

"How?" Rob eyed her carefully.

"Well, he...he just...he called me names. Terrible names. He gave me bruises."

Alvin threw his work hat on the ground. "When? When did I do *any* of that, Cynthia?"

"You grabbed my arm, remember? When you found out about Nate."

"What did you expect me to do? Pick you flowers? A man doesn't take too kindly when he finds out his wife..." Alvin sucked in a sob.

Rob truly felt bad for the man, even if he was the one Cynthia had dumped him for.

"You two need to forgive each other." Rob watched them both.

"I don't think I can forgive her for that. And how do I know she won't do it again?" Alvin shook his head.

"Don't you read the Bible?"

"Of course." Did Alvin take offense to his words?

"*You* need to read Hosea. It's about unconditional love." Rob then turned to Cynthia. "Do *you* remember the story of the woman caught in adultery that was brought before Jesus?"

She nodded.

"Jesus knew she had sinned. He told her to *go and sin no more*." He stared at her to be sure his words registered.

"Listen, I am far from a counselor or a preacher. But for the sake of those *kinner*, you two *need* to work out your differences. This life isn't just about you. You need

92

to forgive each other. And you need to set a good example for your children.

"If God loved you enough to send Jesus to die for you, you should have the decency to not make a mockery of Him."

"What do you mean?" Alvin frowned.

"Jesus Christ hung on that cross so your sins could be forgiven, so you could go to Heaven. It was His gift to all mankind. When we choose our own way by refusing to forgive each other and rejecting His gift, we are telling God and the world that God's love was not enough for us." He blew out a breath. "But God's grace *is* enough to cover *all* our sins. No sin is too big for God to forgive."

Rob shook his head. "I'm going to leave you two to work this out."

He began walking toward the vehicle.

"Rob, wait," Cynthia called, but he ignored her.

He jumped into the car and locked the doors before she got the notion to force her way in.

He rolled down the window a smidgen. "Work it out."

As he drove out of Alvin's driveway, his gaze went to the rearview mirror. Alvin and Cynthia seemed to stand in place, dumbfounded, as they both stared after him.

"God, I hope that was the right thing to do. Please help them to work this out. If You will, give them a Christmas miracle."

TWELVE

As Rob cleared with the flight tower for landing, he uttered a silent prayer. "Thank You for bringing me home safely once again, Lord. Help me put my own faith into practice as I go and talk to the leaders of Janie's community. Amen."

He still hadn't heard anything from Janie, which caused worry and doubt to creep into his heart. Had she changed her mind about flying with him? Had she decided being 'friends' was not an option after all?

Honestly, he couldn't see being just her friend. No. He realized that he wanted something more with Janie. He longed for something deep and lasting.

Holding Cynthia's *boppli* was what had done it. It's what had created a renewed desire for a family of his own. He decided then and there that no matter what the verdict from the elders was, he planned to join their *g'may* and seriously court Janie.

Friendship was not enough.

The thought of giving up flying pained him, but not as much as a future void of a woman's love. He would sacrifice one for the other, if that's what it came to. Wasn't that what love was about? Sacrificing oneself for the sake of another?

Exactly what Jesus did for me. The thought seemed to come out of nowhere. The truth remained. One couldn't have true love without sacrifice.

~

Janie stared at the zero on the answering machine on their store's phone. It had been three days since she'd left messages for Rob. Surely, he would have received one of them by now. She hadn't trusted his ex-girlfriend to relay her message, so she'd called back later and left one on his phone.

Did he feel guilty because he'd been spending time with his ex-girlfriend? If he intended to stay in Pennsylvania until Christmas, she would think that he'd at least call to let her know. Perhaps he'd been too busy to remember that he'd offered to take her flying.

Whatever the case, she just wished he'd communicate with her. She didn't like silence. It allowed doubts to creep in, whether they were unfounded or not.

Sunday wasn't until tomorrow—the day Rob would have taken her flying. She tried not to despair, but it proved difficult. Had she only been imagining their mutual attraction? Had she read him wrong?

As she walked back to the main house, then into her bedroom, her thoughts immediately flew to Rob's jacket. She lifted it from her desk chair and brought it to her nose. Rob's scent enveloped her once again. If nothing else, he'd at least return for his jacket.

At least, she hoped he would.

As afternoon turned into evening, her doubts grew.

~

Rob sat on a couch across from the leaders of Janie's Amish community.

The man who identified himself as Mose Hershberger, who Rob assumed was the bishop, leaned forward. "Joash has come to see us on your behalf."

"Oh. He has?" The fact helped set Rob's mind at ease some.

"Says you're a pilot," Mose lifted a brow.

"That's correct. I'm a flight instructor. I teach others how to fly airplanes." He clasped his hands together.

"And you're interested in joining the *g'may*?" the deacon chimed in.

"That's correct," Rob affirmed.

"Joash said you are interested in his *dochder* Janie. We are worried that a job such as this would take you away from a family." The bishop eyed him thoughtfully.

"Most of my work is during normal hours, just like any other job. However, some night flying is required for the students' certification. If that goes against your wishes, I can have another instructor supervise during the nighttime flights."

Mose looked to the other leaders, who seemed to be mulling the situation over.

"And where do you fly from?"

"Well, currently, I'm about an hour and a half away by car. I plan to move up here, though. I discovered there's a small airport about ten minutes away. When I get my own place, I'd like to have a private landing strip. That is, if it's approved."

"We're concerned this will cause our *youngie* to desire *Englisch* ways." Mose looked to him for an answer.

"I've thought of that, actually. And unless given permission by the leaders, I will not teach any of the Amish to fly." Rob hoped this was an acceptable solution. He'd gone over every possible objection they might have, in his mind, prior to coming.

Mose looked to the other men, then turned back to Rob. "We would like a few moments to discuss this matter privately, if you'd like to step into the kitchen."

"Sure." Rob complied. He'd be praying for a favorable outcome the entire time.

THIRTEEN

"Janie, will you get the door?" Her father called from the kitchen. No doubt, he was preparing his evening tea.

Receiving visitors at this time of night was rare. Had there been an emergency with one of her siblings' families? She hurried to the door and pulled it open.

"Rob?" Her jaw went slack. She'd hoped he'd call, but this...this was a surprise.

His stare was intent. "May we talk privately?"

She swallowed. Was he going to tell her he'd gotten back together with his ex-girlfriend? "*Jah*. Sure. Just a minute."

She rushed into the kitchen intending to ask her father for use of the living room. He'd been all too happy to comply. "Don't worry about me, *dochder*. You two take all the time you need. I've got my tea and a copy of The Budget to keep me occupied."

"*Denki, Dat*." She smiled and returned to the living room.

Rob had taken a seat on the couch.

"May I get you a snack?" She offered. Yikes, if she didn't have misgivings about his ex-girlfriend, this would have felt like they were courting. The two of them alone in the living room. Her offering him a snack.

"No, thank you. At least, not right now. Will you come sit?" He patted space next to him.

She nodded and joined him on the sofa. Being close to Rob did funny things to her insides.

"I have so much to tell you." He reached for her hand. "But first..." he sighed. Was he nervous? "Will you let me court you?"

A knock upside the head with a frying pan couldn't have astonished her more. "You want to court *me*?" It hadn't been until that moment that she noticed he was wearing Amish clothing, sans the hat and hairstyle.

"If you'll let me. I mean, if you want to." He looked so unsure of himself.

But... "What about your ex-girlfriend?"

His brow lowered. "My ex-girlfriend?"

"*Jah*. In Pennsylvania? I called your phone and it sounded like—"

He shook his head. "There is absolutely *nothing* going on with me and my ex-girlfriend." He stopped. "Wait. You called?"

"I did. She answered."

"Ah, that explains it. I forgot my phone at my parents' house when I went to visit my dad in the hospital."

"The hospital?"

"I can see we have a lot to catch up on. Let's talk about it later, okay?

She nodded.

"About my question? Will you let me court you?"

"But, the leaders. And you're still *Englisch, ain't so?*" His thumb lightly roving the top her hand distracted her. She could definitely get used to his touch. *Oh my.*

"I talked to the leaders today. I can join the *g'may* in the spring when baptism classes come around again."

"*Ach*, for real?" Her heartbeat quickened by the second. "That's just a few months away."

He nodded, a full smile on his face now.

"But what about your flying?"

"I can keep my job." He squeezed her hand, his smile growing even more.

"Wow. I can hardly believe it!"

"So, is that a *yes*?" He chuckled.

"*Ach*, for sure. It is one hundred percent a yes."

"Good. I was hoping you'd say something like that." He reached up and touched her cheek, his gaze swathing her face in a caress. She was certain that longing sparked in his eyes.

But she knew he wouldn't kiss her yet. She'd likely have to wait until they'd courted a while. Either way was fine with her, but she preferred sooner rather than later.

"Is your father here?"

"He's in the kitchen."

"Should we go share the news with him?"

"Yes!"

They both rose from the couch. Hand-in-hand, they walked into the kitchen. Janie was sure they were both beaming—possibly even radiating physical light.

"Heard every word." Her father grinned.

"*Dat*!" Janie gasped. "You weren't supposed to be eavesdropping."

"I live a boring life, *dochder*. Will you rob me of this one simple pleasure?" She didn't buy his sheepish look for one minute.

Rob chuckled, then stretched his hand toward her father. "Thank you for speaking to the leaders on my behalf."

"*Ach*, you did? What did you say?" Janie hadn't a clue her father had been in contact with the church leaders.

Her father ignored her question and looked to Rob. "All went well, then?"

"*Jah*. I can hardly believe they're letting me keep my job. But they said if it causes problems, I'll have to find a different occupation." He shrugged. "And in the future my night flights will go to another instructor so I can be home in the evenings."

Janie detected the unspoken words *with my family*. But that wouldn't come until after marriage. Anticipation surged through her entire being.

~

Rob pulled Janie close to his chest, enclosing her in his oversized coat. Their breath swirled upward in the chilly night air. He rested his cheek on top of her head, enjoying her nearness. She felt so good in his arms.

"Do you think your *dat* will be all right?" He loved the fact that Janie was concerned about his father, but he didn't want to talk about that during the final moments of their evening together.

"I think so. But we can discuss that another time. We only have a few minutes together before I leave. I want to think about us."

"I'm still in shock, I think." She stared up at him, her eyes sparkling under the moonlight.

"And *I* think I might kiss you. Would that be too forward of me?"

"*Ach, nee*. I...hoped you would." A shy smile graced her lips.

He chuckled. "Really?"

At her nod, he lowered his mouth to hers. The softness of her lips, the gentleness of her touch as her fingers intertwined with the hair at the nape of his neck, and her nearness caused him to tremble.

The excitement of kissing Janie had to be akin to the thrill of jumping out of an airplane with only a parachute on your back. Pure exhilaration.

He didn't want this perfect night to end. He pulled back, but kept her close. "I have an idea. Would you like to take a drive?"

Her gaze meandered to his face. "Right now?"

"Yeah." He couldn't hide his smile if he tried.

She shrugged. "Sure. I'll need to run in and let *Dat* know so he doesn't worry about me."

"Okay. I'll warm up the truck." He reluctantly released her, then moved to his truck and turned over the ignition. The nights had been frigid lately, so he'd been using the heater non-stop.

That would change once he was required to give up his truck. But a buggy would have its own benefits—the main one being the narrow bench seat where cuddling with Janie was pretty much guaranteed.

A moment later, Janie slid into the passenger's side of the truck, the glimmer in her eye probably just as bright as his.

"You ready?" He regretted having the center console in between them. He missed the older models where your sweetheart could sidle up to you.

"*Jah.*"

He reached over the console and intertwined his fingers with hers. At least they'd still be able to hold hands. "Does your father want you home at a certain time?"

"*Nee*, he said to take our time. He was going to bed."

He pulled out of the driveway and onto the road. "Good. Because we have a little ways to drive."

"Where are we going?"

"That, my love, is a surprise." He stole a glance at her and winked.

~

Janie must've stepped out of a lovely dream. Either that, or she was in the midst of one. It was the only explanation she had for her current circumstances.

Just like that, when she thought she would never marry, *Der Herr* brought along the perfect man. Never, even in her wildest dreams, would she have pictured herself with an airplane pilot. *Ach*, was that where Rob was taking her? Did he even fly airplanes at this time of night?

"I see the wheels in your head turning. We'll be there soon." He reached over and brushed her cheek.

Jah, she must be dreaming. "What are you doing for Christmas?"

"I'll be in Pennsylvania. My mom wanted me to invite you to come along. Do you think you'd be able to?" He glanced her way.

"We usually go to my sister's. Let me ask *Dat* and see what he says."

"I'd love for you to meet my family. And I know they'd love to meet you."

"You can meet mine too. Maybe for Second Christmas?"

"That would work. We'd fly out to Pennsylvania. Are you okay with that?"

She grinned. "It sounds like an adventure."

"It will be."

Excitement bubbled in her belly. "So, where are we going?"

"You'll see. Close your eyes, we're almost there."

"Seriously?"

"Yep. Right now. I don't want to ruin it."

"Okay." She squeezed her eyes closed, wondering what Rob's surprise was.

"You ready?"

"*Jah.* If you are."

"Okay, open your eyes."

Janie's eyes widened and her jaw dropped as she delighted in the colorful Christmas lights all around them. "Oh, my goodness. How many lights are there?"

"Over a million, I believe. Listen." He reached over and turned on the radio."

She giggled. "They're flashing with the music. *Ach,* this is *wunderbaar*!"

109

"I hoped you'd like it. Have you ever been before?"

"No. Never. Where are we?"

"This is Indy. The fairgrounds."

"Indianapolis?"

He nodded.

"How did you find out about this?"

"I saw a short clip on the news. I knew it was going to be great, but this...this is awesome."

"It's your first time too?"

"Yep." He reached for her hand. "I'd hoped to enjoy it with someone special. If we want to do this in the future, we'll have to hire a driver."

Ach, he was talking about the future—their future—as though it were a sure thing. Dare she dream of one day being married to Rob?

FOURTEEN

Rob helped Joash stock t-shirts on a shelf in the new souvenir section of the store, while Janie tended to customers at the bakery counter.

"You know, it's nice having an extra set of hands around," Janie's father commented.

Rob chuckled. "I can't seem to stay away."

"Like honey to a bear, I suppose." Joash grinned, placing keychains on a revolving rack. "You are *gut* for my *dochder*."

"And she's good for me. It's strange, isn't it? How an unexpected Christmas gift could draw two strangers together."

"Did you two ever solve your mystery?"

"No. The candy company won't divulge any information. I'll just consider it a gift from God. I don't know if Janie and I would have met otherwise."

"A Christmas miracle for both of you."

"You know, I've never thought of it that way. But that's the perfect way to describe it." He pulled a stack of magnets out of the cardboard box and strategically placed them on the metal side of the spinning rack.

"I haven't seen *mei dochder* this happy in a long time. I'm trusting you to take *gut* care of her."

"I plan to."

Joash disappeared to help a customer check out.

Rob strained to catch a glimpse of Janie, but the shelves were in the way. He'd love to sneak off into the back of the store with her and indulge in a kiss or two. He felt a lopsided grin forming as he acted on the impulse, abandoning his shelving duties. They could wait.

Just his good fortune. There were no customers in sight. He dashed behind the bakery counter and pulled Janie through the double doors that led to the kitchen.

She giggled. "What are you doing?"

The doors closed behind them and he pulled her out of view into the pantry, lest anyone should walk in. He yanked on the light string that hung above them, thankful Janie's modern Amish district allowed their businesses to use electricity.

"I couldn't wait another minute." When he read the enthusiasm dancing in her eyes, he leaned close and brushed her lips with his, trapping her between the pantry door and himself. To his delight, she responded with a zeal of her own. *Ach*, he yearned for the day when the two of them would be married.

But they weren't yet.

He forced himself away, certain his mien must be giving away his intoxicated state of mind.

"That was...nice." Janie giggled.

He couldn't help himself as he bent toward her and claimed another kiss, then broke away. "Janie, you...you drive me crazy."

She smiled. "I hope that's a *gut* thing."

He chuckled. "It's good and bad at the same time."

Her head shot up. "*Ach*, I think—"

"Janie?" The door swung open and Joash stood on the other side. "What are you two—?" His eyes darted back and forth from Janie to Rob as realization dawned on him.

Janie's cheeks were aflame with color, and Rob was certain his must be as well.

"We just...uh, we should get back to work." Rob swallowed.

Joash frowned. "*Jah*, you should. Especially since the deacon is waiting at the counter." His brow hitched.

"*Ach.*" Janie shot a worried look at Rob. "I'll go help him."

Janie squeezed past Rob and he watched her disappear through the double doors, leaving him alone with her father.

"Do we need to talk?" Joash's scrutinizing gaze caused Rob to squirm internally.

Rob shook his head.

"I'm guessing you were doing more than *talking* behind the closed door."

Rob nodded. "We were."

"I'm not convinced it's a *gut* idea for *mei dochder* to go with you to Pennsylvania." Joash crossed his arms over his chest.

Oh no. "You're welcome to come along."

"In an airplane?"

"We could drive, but it would take much longer. And flying is safer. A lot less traffic up there." He pointed up.

"It is *Der Herr* who keeps each one safe, regardless of the mode of transportation."

"You're right. And whether you go along or not, I promise not to overstep my bounds with Janie. We'll be staying with my folks."

Joash reached over and squeezed Rob's shoulder. "I trust you to do what's right. And don't believe for a minute that I didn't steal a kiss or two from Janie's *mamm* before we were hitched." He winked.

Rob chuckled. "Did you get a talking-to from her father too?"

"Can't say we ever got caught." His eyes twinkled.

FIFTEEN

While the sights and sounds of soaring thousands of feet above the ground was thrilling, Janie looked forward to the safety of having her feet firmly planted on the ground.

"You okay?" Rob smiled from the cockpit, his voice crystal clear through the headset she wore.

"*Jah*. It's exciting." She peered out the window as the clouds moved under them. "How long before we land?"

He chuckled. "A little nervous?"

"Just a little. I'm glad you know what you're doing, because I have no clue."

"Don't you worry. If this wasn't safe I wouldn't have brought you up." He reached over and squeezed her hand. "I can't wait for you to meet my family."

"Me too." She grinned.

"I imagine I will look ridiculous to anyone who sees me." He glanced down at his attire.

"Not every day you see an Amish man flying an airplane." She giggled.

"My family hasn't seen me in Amish clothes in quite some time. They just might think you're an angel." He winked.

"I doubt that." She laughed and poked his ribs.

"You're the answer to their prayers. You have rescued the lost sheep. They are going to love you."

"So, do they already know that you're joining the church?"

He shook his head. "I wanted it to be a surprise. And I wanted to tell them in person. Since my father's stroke, they've had a lot to deal with. This will bring smiles to their faces."

"That makes me happy."

"Good. I want you to be happy. I want to make you happy for the rest of your life."

She smiled. "I understand what you mean. But we must depend on *Gott* for our contentment."

"You're right, of course. I just meant that I want to do everything within my power to keep you smiling. I love your smile."

"*Ach*, Rob. You're flattering me."

"I'm just telling the truth, is all." He checked his instruments. "You ready to descend?"

She sucked in a breath. "Ready as I'll ever be."

~

Walking toward the parking area, excitement jolted through Rob's insides as he reached for Janie's hand. He couldn't wait to see the look on his family's face when they saw him.

Dressed in Amish clothing.

With a beautiful young woman at his side.

Whom he hoped to marry as soon as the leaders would allow.

He scanned the tiny parking area just without the airport's fence, but no driver awaited them. They appeared to be the only people in sight. He specifically told Mom he did *not* want Cynthia to pick them up.

"Looks like we'll have to wait a bit. Maybe I should have rented a vehicle."

Janie laughed. "If you're joining the church, you probably want to start getting used to being without a car, ain't so?"

"You're right. I've gotten spoiled with being able to jump into my truck or the plane to go wherever I want."

Janie frowned. "Are you sure and certain that's what you want to do?"

He wanted to kiss the worry right off her face. He reached over and caressed her cheek instead. "Without a doubt."

Could an airplane carry on an intelligent conversation and filled his heart with gladness? Could a truck snuggle up with him and keep him warm at night? He chuckled to himself at his silly thoughts.

"What?" Janie smiled.

He shook his head. "I'm just so happy to have you in my life, that's all. I'm still a little stunned at all that's happened within the past few weeks."

"It is a pretty crazy situation. I never thought I'd meet someone like you. I never even dreamed that I'd be flying in an airplane at Christmastime—or at any time at all, for that matter."

"God knew how much I needed you." He bent down and grazed the tip of her nose with his lips.

"And how much *I* needed *you*." She lifted her face to meet his lips with hers.

Just as a vehicle pulled up. He broke away at the sound of tires churning on the asphalt.

"Oh, no. I hope my mom isn't in there. I'll get a lecture on PDA for sure and certain." He winked at Janie.

But it wasn't his mom. It was Cynthia. Again.

He sighed. Exactly what he *didn't* want.

Rob hurried to the vehicle before Cynthia had the chance to burst out and engulf him in an embrace like she had last time. He was pretty certain that Janie's presence wouldn't deter her. He opened the back door for Janie and then slid in beside her.

"Thanks for the ride." He ground out the words.

Janie eyed him curiously.

Cynthia's face peered into the rearview mirror, then she turned slightly. "I'm the ex." Her eyes flitted from Janie to Rob. "Sorry. Your parents' driver wasn't available. Since I still had the car and I was next door, I volunteered."

Cynthia backed out of the parking lot and maneuvered the vehicle onto the road.

He nodded, not wanting to get into a conversation with Cynthia, especially with Janie present.

She continued, "I'm not living with my folks anymore. The *kinner* and I moved back in with Alvin." She swallowed. "I have you to thank for that."

He nodded once and hard. "I'm glad to hear it. And save your thanks for God."

"Oh, I have thanked Him many times. But it was *your* words that shook sense into Alvin and me. We're working it out." She caught Janie's eye through the mirror again. Tears shimmered in her eyes. "Don't let him go. He's a keeper."

Janie glanced at him and he smiled, lacing his fingers though hers.

"I don't plan to," Janie said.

SIXTEEN

The door to Rob's parents' house swung open the second he and Janie stepped onto the porch.

"You're here, *sohn*!" His mother positively beamed. "And you brought someone?" Her smile widened even more at the sight of Janie, if that were possible.

Rob grinned and squeezed Janie's hand. "Mom, this is Janie, the girl I told you about."

"Wonderful!" She pulled Janie into an embrace. "It's so *gut* to finally meet you. Rob told us all about you."

Janie glanced at him, amusement dancing on her lips. "He did?"

"All good things, for sure and certain," his mother assured. She looked back at Rob and surveyed his Amish clothing. "Does this...mean something?"

Rob nodded. "I'm joining the *g'may* where Janie and her father attend."

"*Ach*, your *vatter's* going to be thrilled. Come, let's go share the news with him." She pulled them from the foyer as soon as they divested themselves of their scarves, gloves, and coats.

"How's he doing?"

"Much better, thanks to your research. We see improvement with every therapy session." She patted his hand.

"I'm happy to hear that."

"Look who's here!" His mother rushed to a recliner where his father rested. He did indeed appear more spry than when Rob last visited.

Dad smiled. "Robert. And who is this?"

Rob urged Janie forward as he pressed the small of her back. "This is Janie. My *schatzi*." He winked at her.

Janie offered her hand and encased it in both of his. "Welcome to the family, *dochder*."

Rob shot an apologetic look at Janie, whose cheeks had blossomed into a deep shade of crimson. "No, Dad. We're just dating right now. She's not...we're not...at least, not yet." *Ach*, he was making a mess of things!

His mother laughed. "He knows, Robert. I believe he's just hoping for the best."

"You guys are going to scare her away." He squeezed Janie's hand.

"Oh, I don't think she'd scare away that easily. Would you, Janie?" Mom smiled.

Janie shook her head. "I'm afraid you might be stuck with me."

"Oh, I'd be happy to be stuck with you." Rob winked. "Hey, isn't that a song?"

Janie and Mom both shrugged.

"Never mind." Rob chuckled.

"Let me show you two to your rooms."

Janie turned back to his father. "It was nice meeting you."

"Oh, you'll get more time with him before you leave. Bill plays a mean game of Connect Four and he won't let anyone escape without playing a round or two."

"I like Connect Four." Janie smiled at his dad. "And I'm pretty good at it too."

"Oh, oh, oh, Bill. It looks like you might have a formidable opponent." His mother warned.

"Bring it on," Dad's eyes sparkled, then focused on Rob. "I like this one, Robert."

Rob pulled Janie close to his side. "Me too, Dad."

~

Janie was certain her heart couldn't be fuller. This visit with Rob's family, although it wouldn't last nearly long enough for her liking, had been *wunderbaar*.

She didn't know if she'd ever remember all of Rob's relatives. In just his immediate family, he had five brothers and six sisters, and there was each one's spouse and *kinner*. She'd have Rob write down a list for her when they got back home. But without photos, she'd have a difficult time remembering who was who.

His siblings had teased him relentlessly about the prodigal returning home, but it was all in good fun.

"Robert, will you and Janie get the door, please? I think that's your *Aentie* Sarah bringing the dessert."

"Sure thing, Mom." He pulled the door open. "Merry Christmas!"

"*Frehlicher Grishtdaag* to you, dear Robert! What a pleasure to see you home." *Aentie* Sarah engulfed him in a hug. She then unabashedly assessed his clothing. "Does this mean you've returned? Or...wait." Her gaze moved to beyond him where Janie stood.

Rob smiled, knowing she'd have more to say.

"I see you've brought someone with you."

"I did." Rob grinned, pulling Janie forward.

Surprise registered on his aunt's face. "You look very familiar. I *know* that I know you from somewhere."

"*Auntie* Sarah, this is Janie Mishler. She lives in Indiana."

"*Ach*! I knew that you looked familiar! Mishler's Bakery, right?"

"*Jah*." Janie nodded with a smile.

"I was in your shop a few months back, do you remember? You helped me find the local Amish directory and some of that herbal ointment you sell. I bought the most delicious chocolate ~* from you." Her hand shot into the air. "Which reminds me. Did you ever receive the chocolates I sent?"

"You sent me chocolates?" Janie's brow furrowed and she turned to look at Rob.

"I did. In fact, I sent some to Robert as well." She frowned at her nephew. "Which I'm still waiting for a Thank-You card for."

"Wait." Rob chuckled. "You sent a box of chocolate to Janie? And to me?"

Aentie Sarah nodded.

"I think we may have solved our mystery." He smiled at Janie.

His aunt's gaze darted back and forth between them. "What are you talking about? What mystery?"

Rob and Janie proceeded to tell her the entire story, as they led her to the living room.

"So, they must've got mixed up somehow. It seems to me like the candy company owes you a box of chocolates, young man." *Aentie* Sarah plopped down on the couch next to Rob.

"They've given me something much better." He draped his arm around Janie's shoulders. By the look in his eye, he wanted a kiss.

"Now I know why I never received a Thank-You note from either of you." *Aentie* Sarah shook her head. "Never underestimate the power of prayer."

"What do you mean?"

"When I placed that order for your chocolates, I prayed that *Gott* would somehow use my gift to bring you back into the fold." She smiled down at Rob and Janie's intertwined hands. "And it looks like that's exactly what He's done. Now I can open up my prayer box and move that prayer to the answered prayer box."

"Prayer box?"

"Oh, yes. Something my *mamm* taught me as young *maedel*. She gave me special box and told me that when I wanted to beseech *Gott* for something to write my prayer out on a scrap of paper while I'm asking Him. Then she told me to place the prayer into the box. When *Gott* would answer one of the prayers, she said to move it to the answered prayers box.

"You know, it's amazing how *Der Herr* listens to us. Even if we think it's something small that He might not care about, we should go to Him. I've found He cares about the little things just as much as the big things."

Rob's brows rose. "Hmm...do they all get answered?"

"Some are answered right away, others have been in the box for years. Sometimes *Gott* says yes, and sometimes He says no. But He always answers...eventually."

Excitement bubbled in Janie's chest. "It sounds like a wonderful thing to do! I think I'll start when we get back home."

SEVENTEEN

"I think it was a *gut* idea to spend Christmas Eve and Christmas day with your family." Janie glanced back at Rob as she stirred the melting chocolate on the stove.

He crept up behind her and slipped his arms around her waist as she prepared dessert for this evening. "And Second Christmas with yours." He murmured in her ear, then brushed his lips to her earlobe.

If she wasn't worried about scalding the chocolate, she'd turn in his arms and indulge in a kiss or two.

"What are you making?"

"The dessert your aunt was talking about."

"May I help?"

"Sure."

He moved to the side, his eyes sparking with mischief as he dipped his finger into the chocolate, then smudged her cheek.

"Hey!" She feigned frustration, even though she enjoyed every second of Rob's teasing. "We're going to need every drop of that chocolate."

"Oh, I won't let it go to waste." A coy smile played on his lips as he leaned close and *very* slowly kissed the place he'd smeared the chocolate.

A bolt of electricity traveled up her spine and it took her a few seconds to recover. "You..." –she caught her breath— "...you planned that, didn't you?"

"Maybe." He moved to the sink and washed his hands. "But I do want to help. Put me to work, baby."

"Baby? I think you've been in the *Englisch* world too long." She shook her head and laughed.

Her head snapped around as footsteps entered the kitchen. "*Dat.*"

"Just checking to make sure this *bu* is behaving himself." Her father eyed Rob.

"He isn't."

Rob gasped in mock horror. "*Ach. Me?* Not behaving?"

"Imagine that." *Dat* shook his head. "*Kumm, bu.* I have something to keep you out of *mei dochder's* hair."

"What's that?"

"We need more wood for the fire."

"That, I can do." Rob followed her father out of the kitchen, but not before turning back and staring longingly at Janie.

Janie smiled to herself as the door to the mudroom closed behind them.

"*Denki, Gott,* for blessing my life with Rob," she whispered.

After all she'd lost when Elson died, never had she dared to dream that love would find her again. What if this was all a dream? What if this was just a test of some sort? What would she do if something happened to Rob and she lost him too?

Janie allowed her mind to descend into that dark excruciating place—the days and weeks and months following Elson's death. So many of her hopes and dreams had been buried in Elson's casket with him. But they'd resurrected when she'd met Rob.

If she were to lose Rob...

She couldn't help the sob that escaped her lips, nor the tears that followed. Maybe she shouldn't have opened up her heart to love again. Maybe it would be easier to live without love than to chance devastation again. Maybe...

"Janie, what wrong?" Rob. She hadn't even heard him walk back into the kitchen. The concern in Rob's voice was nearly her undoing.

"I don't know if I can do this." She sobbed.

Rob rushed to her and gathered her in his arms. "Do what, baby?"

"Us."

He pulled back and whisked away her tears under his thumbs. "What do you mean?"

"I love you. If anything were to ever happen to you..." She hated herself for crying so much.

"Hey. Hey, now." He lifted her chin and lightly brushed his lips to hers. "It's all right, Janie. God's got this, okay? Do you think He would have gone through all that trouble to send you chocolates from me if He was just going to snatch me away?"

How did Rob always know the right thing to say?

Janie couldn't help the giggle that tripped from her lips. "No, I imagine not."

The steady beat of his heart echoed in her ear. She could stay in his arms forever.

"Our time is in His hands. We have to trust Him. And I sincerely doubt that He would have us meet and then leave one of us heartbroken." His fingers caressed her jaw.

He stepped away. "I came in here to get you. Your sister and brothers and their families just pulled up."

Excitement bubbled inside Janie as she thought of the wonderful evening ahead. Her siblings would no doubt love Rob.

He pulled her by the hand toward the living room. "*Kumm*, you need to introduce them to your Heaven-sent future husband." He winked.

Janie sighed in contentment. Heaven-sent indeed.

EPILOGUE

Christmas Eve Day, two years later...

Rob dipped the washcloth into the water and dabbed his *fraa's* forehead. Janie still lounged in the inflatable tub, where she'd birthed their second *boppli*, a *maedel*, several moments before.

"She did a *wunderbaar* job. You should be proud, *sohn*." Rob's mother smiled as she handed their little one to her daddy.

"*Ach*, she's just as beautiful as her *mamm*." Rob knelt close to the tub and kissed Janie's cheek. "Isn't she perfect?"

Tears shimmered in Janie's eyes. "She is."

"What should we name her?" He had a difficult time taking his eyes off his brand-new baby girl as he gently stroked her impossibly soft skin.

"Knock. Knock." Janie's father Joash called out from behind the bedroom door. "Is it safe to come in? We're dying to see that new *boppli*."

"Come on in." Janie's smile stretched across her face.

Their one-year-old son, Little Joe, named after Joash, reached for Rob.

"Looks like someone might be jealous," Joash said.

"Nah." Rob's mother batted a hand in front of her. "He just wants to see his new baby sister and make sure his daddy hasn't forgotten him."

Rob held both of their children. "What do you think of your new sister?"

Little Joe hesitantly touched the baby's head, his eyes widening.

"Oh! I forgot to tell you." Joash eyed Rob and Janie. "Something just came for you two." He handed them a package, his eyes twinkling.

"What is it?" Rob handed the baby to Joash, then shook the package. "Want to help me open this, bud?" He asked Little Joe. "I think your mama's hands are wet."

With Little Joe's help, he pulled the kraft wrapping paper from the package. "Look, LJ, it's a box of chocolates. I can't imagine who these might be from." He winked at his *fraa*.

"*Ach*! I know it." Janie smiled.

"Know what?"

"What we can name the *boppli*. How about we name her after your *Aentie* Sarah?"

"Little Sarah?" He thought on it. "I like it."

"I think that's the perfect name," Rob's mother said.

"And appropriate, since she gave you both your Christmas miracle." Joash said.

"*Nee*, the miracle came from *Der Herr*. He just prompted my aunt to send us chocolate." He held out the box to Janie. "Indulge, my love. You deserve it more than anyone."

Rob bent down and kissed his *fraa's* lips. Who would have thought that their miracle could come through a box of chocolates—from an unexpected Christmas gift?

Grab another story for free when you sign up for my newsletter at www.jenniferspredemann.com

THE END

Thanks for reading! To GOD be the glory!

www.ingramcontent.com/pod-product-compliance
Lightning Source LLC
Chambersburg PA
CBHW011435170626
46808CB00010B/3179